PERVERTED ANALYTICAL SHY OUT

NON QUESTIONABLE QUESTIONING SPOKEN

ATHLETIC CONFUSED RECLUSIVE

NERD PEANUT

RELIGIOUS

INTRO EDUCATED

VERTED

D I F F E R E N T

TITTY ROMANTIC NEGLECTED

B A B Y GROWTH

ABRAHM TURNER

MY SO CALLED LIFE, ITS MY TURN TO SPEAK

This book is a work of fiction.
Any persons or events that are similar to actual events or
persons are only a matter of coincidence.

Address all inquiries to:
Abrahm Turner
abewrites16@gmail.com

ISBN-13: 978-0692815953
Printed in the United States of America
Houston, Texas 77003

LIFE IS A SERIES OF ACTIONS
DEFINED BY WORDS MADE UP OF MANY LETTERS, EACH LETTER IS A
MERE FRACTION OF WHO I AM, WHERE I HAVE
GONE AND WHO I HAVE BECOME.

TABLE OF CONTENTS

INTRODUCTION

DEDICATION

5
CHAPTER ONE

In The Beginning…

14
CHAPTER TWO

When I Was A Child…

33
CHAPTER THREE
Look to the Hills…

48
CHAPTER FOUR

Judge Not…

63
CHAPTER FIVE

Blessed Is The Man…

76
CHAPTER SIX

Peace Be Still…

INTRODUCTION

To begin, I am young adult who decides to write a book, at a plateau in my life. I aspire to do many things in my lifetime, most importantly, to write this book and to complete my college education. I am confident that this book will spark dialogue about some of the troubles and truths about being a child, trying to become an adult. This book will allow the audience to visualize the adversities and obstacles, as well as the triumphs that youths experience. Sit back and revisit the pathways of the life of young Christopher Coldwell, witness his beginnings, feel his struggles and come to understand the pivotal points in "My So-Called Life. " These are only the struggles and triumphs that make us all human. Please listen up because it's his turn to speak. Enjoy!

DEDICATION AND THANKS

I dedicate this book to my mother. I want to thank you
for always being that light, when the path I traveled
seemed so dark.

I also, give an honor to God Almighty for bestowing
upon me the wisdom and knowledge to make it
through the valley.

I would like to send a special thanks to my good friend
and "play" brother Josh as without him this book
would not have been possible.

Finally, for others who were near and kind, I want to say
thanks. I want to thank those who were that listening-ear in
my life when I just needed to vent without charging me one
dime of counseling time. I want to also thank Gloria for
inspiring me to finish this book, and for just being a friend.

MY SO CALLED LIFE, ITS MY TURN TO

SPEAK

CHAPTER ONE

IN THE BEGINNING

"I'm fine and sexy now, Deuce. I have finally lost all them pounds Tyson packed on me."

Tyson was my first swing at having a child, much less raising one, and it took me years to lose all the baby weight. He's almost five now, so I can finally let him out of my sight for a moment. He's already reading, and talking in full sentences.

"Hey Foxy, let's go out t'night." grumbled Deuce.

"Who's gonna keep Tyson?" I asked.

"We can drop him off at Ms. Josephine's house."

"That'll be fine. Besides, Mama always takes good care of him," I agreed.

"Hey Mama, we'll be back to pick up Tyson around midnight, okay?"

"That's fine Foxy, y'all go enjoy yourselves."

"Foxy, baaaby, it is packed tonight! Hey waiter, can we get some service here?"

"May I help y'all?"

"I'll have a Crown and Coke."

"And for you, ma'am?"

"I'd like a Canadian Mist and 7-Up, please."

"Will that be all?"

"Yea, for right now."

"Hey Deuce, I'm really glad to be out. We hardly go out anymore because all the overtime you're required to put in at the lumber mill."

"Huh? Foxy, did you say something?"

"Yea I did, but your eyes and ears were over there, with that other woman."

"Huh, what did you say?"

"Oh, nothing." Deuce was a bit of a womanizer. "Hey! Deuce, listen to me!"

"Uh, I'm listening, what?"

"Why did you do it?"

"I dunno, I just got caught up in the moment I guess. Besides, it was a mutual thing."

I can't begin to tell you why I was with that man for so long, then I looked over at him and I began to smile a bit.

Deuce was a man of misguided love, but he was a hard worker, a provider, and a man of good intentions—or at least that's what I told myself. I really couldn't blame him for catching all the attention he got, 'cause he was twenty-six, had mocha-brown skin, and a deep baritone voice that'd make you melt. On top of it all, he was six feet tall, with big hands and big feet. Y'all know what I'm talking about. But hey, don't get it wrong. Deuce wasn't the only good-looking person in the relationship. After all, he did catch me, Ms. Foxy. I was quite the brick house. Thanks to my mom and dad for the good hair and genes. With long silky hair and this Coca-Cola bottle-shaped figure, what man wouldn't want me by his side? I was the total package, but what can I say, I was in love with my womanizing man.

"Here's your drinks."

I stared at my pale drink as it sat on its clean, dry napkin, bubbling enthusiastically at me. The feeling wasn't mutual.

"Um, waiter, could I get something a little stronger?"

"Okay, sure. What will you have?"

"I'll have two stiff shots of Johnny Walker Red, and one country club malt liquor, please."

"Are you sure, ma'am? That's an awful lot of alcohol for a young lady."

With a scowl etched into my face I shouted, "Hey, just get it okay!" I hate to admit it, but I used alcohol as a buffer to self-medicate for the tiny person crying out within. It was just a temporary fix though. I was just tryin' to handle my "ordinary pain," aka Deuce. Seemed not to hurt as much when I was drinking.

ONE MONTH LATER

"Hey Deuce, you are never going to guess what I found out t'day. I'm pregnant!" Just when I thought I was done with this stuff.

With surprise, and an awkward yet happy look smeared across his face. "Are you sure, Foxy?"

"Yea, I haven't seen my cycle in a month, and besides, I took a test. It came back positive."

"Well Foxy, at least we're moving out of this shack into our own house in two months."

"Deuce, once the test came back positive, I started to do some thinking about making some changes in my life. I decided to quit smoking and drinking. I have to think about our child now."

"Yea, that's right, you do."

As time rolled on I was slowly losing that cute figure it took five years to regain.

"Deuce, in six months I've gained so much weight!" Being pregnant made me fat.

"Foxy, you still look fine to me, baby."

The next three months passed very quickly, and in June of 1981, I was as big as a house. I started having minor labor pains every now and then, but it was nothing I worried about. I was more concerned about giving Deuce a birthday he'd never forget. He was about to be twenty-seven. I wanted ever so desperately to have this baby on his special day. It'd be a gift from me to him. The days passed very quickly, and on the dawn of June 7th I awoke with an extreme level of energy. Already having had my experience with Tyson five years ago, I knew all the tricks of the trade to induce labor. And to think women these days gotta have drugs. I became very determined to push this baby out on this day. I cleaned the house from top to bottom. I even raked some leaves that had fallen from our chinaberry and our pecan tree. I felt pains all over, but none were the real thing. At eight o'clock that night I was rushed to Kittyhawk County Memorial Hospital. My water finally broke with some assistance, and it wasn't Johnny Walker this time.

My doctor readied me for the actual energy draining, painful process, and shortly afterward Deuce arrived. He cleaned up and put on the extra scrubs to assist the doctor. Deuce was always good for that. The doctor told Deuce to assist me in some breathing exercises. I remember like it was yesterday. It was six short breaths. Hee, Hee, Hee, Hah, Hah, Hah. I had to do this over and over again. Ladies, if you have ever had a child you know exactly what I mean. I laughed during the practice because Deuce was making the funniest faces trying to imitate the doctor's breathing instructions. No more laughing that day though, all I could think about was having this baby on June 7th before midnight, but it didn't happen.

On June 8th, 1981 at 5:15 a.m. I gave birth to a handsome baby boy. This pregnancy was somewhat easier than the first because I knew what to expect. I knew if I got pregnant, I would eat everything in sight, gain weight, go into labor and then have the baby in short order. I was glad I was able to have both my children naturally, but this time I wasn't sure about a name. I had thought of some, but I didn't like them. Deuce wanted a namesake, Thomas Coldwell III. Oh, no, no, no. I was surely not going to punish my son with that name. I could only imagine the kids calling him names like Tre or 3. Umm, not on my watch!

I lay quietly in my hospital room, on my warm hospital bed. Then it happened! The perfect name came to me—Christopher. It just appeared right before my eyes.

Perfect, but I still hadn't given Deuce his gift, so I named him Christopher Thomas to pacify him.

The baby was definitely a product of Deuce and me. There was no denying this child; he had my looks to a "T." He was light-skinned with family features, like his nose and feet. He had that famous Lunder nose, big and wide. It was and is a family trademark of sorts. As for his feet, he had my block toes, they had the length of Deuce's toes. That man's toes look like fingers. My toes were short and stubby because as a kid I never had good shoes.

To give a little insight into my childhood, I would often have to cram my feet into shoes that were too small for my wide, growing feet. What can I say, we were poor. I clung to the life Deuce made for me and my babies. It was my escape from the life I had, sharing with my brothers and sisters. Let me be clear, it wasn't just the shoes that defined us as poor. As a kid I learned all too well about how just a little "gov'ment" cheese, buttah, and lite bread made the best-grilled cheese sandwiches.

But let me get back to the story at hand, because talking about my childhood and life would be a book of its own.

I was thrilled to have my second child. Even as a baby I could tell Christopher was very different from his older brother. It wasn't just the five-year age difference, it was something else. I couldn't put my finger on it. Tyson was breastfed about three weeks, then bottled, but not

11

Christopher. This one stayed glued to my breast. All his uncles teased him, calling my baby a "titty baby." Most children stop breastfeeding a few months after being born, but not Christopher. He stayed hooked to my breast until he was almost one year old.

One thing both boys had in common was that they were very intelligent children. Their intelligence far exceeded most children. I thank God for blessing them with intelligence even though they didn't always use it. Christopher, like his big brother Tyson, was making full sentences by the time he was one, and reading by the time he was three. I would practice flash cards with him, and we would watch Sesame Street every day. His favorite characters were the Count and Bert and Ernie. Christopher was most active when he watched the show, but other than that he was a very quiet and reserved child. He always played by himself. He never really associated with the other kids. He never had any friends, real or imaginary, but he was my little "peanut." That was my special nickname for him. Christopher was very intuitive and analytical. He was the type that just sat in the corner of a room and listened. He was very introverted, which was the exact opposite of his brother. He was always around me. He was a mama's boy, and "mama" loved it. The four years after his birth were pretty normal. He had normal birthdays and celebrated holidays, like the rest of the kids.

My marriage was typical. Deuce and I had our arguments like most couples. We never argued about money though—our arguments mostly centered on the rumors that spread around town. Deuce had violated my trust a long time ago, but as most women do, I stayed, determined to make my marriage work. Besides, he was an excellent provider and we never wanted for anything, we had nice clothes and Tyson and Christopher always had the best toys. In hindsight, I know that's not what should have been important. I failed to see the big picture—or maybe I wouldn't allow myself to see. I simply put up with Deuce because we had kids to think about. I know that it was the wrong reason to remain together, because in the end the children became subject to all the negativity. They were affected in ways that would change their lives forever. But I could go on for days, and this is my son's story. I'll turn it over to him now. He remembers all the little details about life that I have forgotten over the years. Most of them I chose to forget. The memories have fallen out of sight. You know how the saying goes, "Out of sight, out of mind."

CHAPTER TWO

WHEN I WAS A CHILD...

The year was 1986, and I was now five years old. Let me begin with fall in September, when everyone was returning to school. I remember it like it was yesterday...

At 6:05 a.m. on September 9th, I was so scared! I got out of bed to get ready, and the fear did not disappear. Even as my mother help me get dressed, I felt butterflies in my stomach, and could not understand why. School was supposed to be fun and exciting. After brushing my teeth and washing my face, my mother made my brother and me line up in the living room for pictures. My mother's nickname should have been Kodak. She got triplicates of every photo she ever took. My brother Tyson stood smiling with that fresh layer of grease on his forehead as Mom snapped his picture. For those who are not in the know, the grease was used to shine up your child to give them that freshly "polished" look. And you know this wasn't just any grease. This was the good stuff that came in those opaque plastic jars with the white lid—petroleum jelly, the kind that provides that "extra shine." I know you're talking bad about us now, but Mom was proud, and she just concentrated on capturing those memories with her camera. Tyson was the epitome of Dad, except for being shorter and having the lighter skin complexion that we both got from Mom. My brother looked fairly well in his picture, but me, I fell victim to my mother's terrible sense of fashion. I was dressed in a plaid green and white shirt, some dark brown pants, and black shoes. Yeah she was wrong, but hey, she tried, right? One out of two ain't bad. I didn't know any better, but even then my clothes seemed like a complete atrocity. I smiled anyway, my own forehead glistening, as Mom snapped my picture.

Soon it was time to go to school in Mom's brown '88 Delta. She asked if I was nervous or scared. My response was no of course, because I was trying to be tough. We arrived at Goldwater Elementary School, and I went right into reserved mode, shy and introverted. Mom walked me to the office, to see who my homeroom teacher was going to be. My teacher was Mrs. Franklin, and although Mrs. Franklin was friendly, I didn't speak to her either. Mrs. Franklin was a white woman in her mid-thirties with a fetish for down-home country dress and she spoke with an educated yet undeniable southern twang. I walked into the room slightly behind my mother, we found my seat, and there I sat, completely silent. When Mom noticed that I had found my place and melted into my surroundings, then she said her good-byes and left. I was now all alone, in a room full of people that I had never seen nor met before. Feeling a bit reclusive, I did not say a word. I just sat there with a forlorn lost sheep look on my face. I don't know how I did it, but I made it through day one. After the first day, I realized very quickly that this was going to be much easier than I had previously thought. School was a breeze for me, and life was good. The school days came and went. After a while, school was just routine, but it wouldn't be long until the repetitiveness was broken.

One day about mid-April, Tyson came down with the chicken pox. I found joy in poking fun at Tyson. He was just itching and scratching like a flea-bitten dog. It was especially funny when he got all covered with calamine lotion, that pink anti-itch cream. Mom, being the kind caretaker that she was, nursed him back to health in no time, but as Tyson got better it happened to me. I was so busy laughing at his misfortune that I caught it from him. This was absolutely the worst time for me to have this awful disease. I had to miss the best and last three weeks of kindergarten. Chicken pox was the worst. Mom made me rest and I was always covered with the pink stuff. I could deal with the itch better than the lotion, because it made my skin smell like a sanitized hospital room. My case of chicken pox was worse than Tyson's. I had it everywhere except my tongue, but finally I prevailed and was better soon enough. Summertime came and life was great again, no more bumps, no more itching or scratching, and best of all, no more calamine lotion. Life couldn't have been better, or so I thought.

One night in early August, Mom started having severe abdominal pains. At midnight on August 4th, Dad rushed Mom to the emergency room at Kittyhawk County Memorial. As her stomach pains increased, several doctors concluded that her appendix must have ruptured and it should be removed immediately. That fateful night, Mom underwent an emergency appendectomy to remove her appendix. During the surgery, the surgeons realized that Mom's true pain was due to a major blockage in her colon. The doctors, realizing their mistake, completed the exploratory appendectomy and hospitalized her for seven days to heal and prepare for the surgery on her colon. As the days progressed, Mom's condition worsened, and on day seven she underwent yet another surgery. Mom was in critical condition, and several times during and after the surgery was on the verge of dying. She was diagnosed with colon cancer and remained hospitalized. As Mom's condition wavered, the small sense of normalcy at home was disrupted. I thought life couldn't get any worse, but it did.

Dad became a member of the Kingdom Hall. The Kingdom Hall, for those of you who are unaware, is the place of worship and fellowship for Jehovah's Witnesses. Holidays were no longer celebrated in our home. No more Halloween, Thanksgiving, Christmas, Easter, or birthdays for us. This was an awful change for my brother and me. Mom didn't convert but we weren't allowed to celebrate with her or attend church services either. I felt life couldn't get any more complex.

Fall rolled in and it was time to return to school. Mom was still hospitalized, so we did not have pictures that year. Mom must have missed taking pictures of Tyson and me. That had always been special to her. Needless to say, we were all starting to miss a lot of things. On the twenty-first day of her hospital stay, Mom was transported to Granville C. Morton Hospital in Dallas, Texas to undergo chemotherapy. Despite the adverse effects that chemotherapy was supposed to have on the body, Mom's hair grew longer and she even gained weight. We made weekend trips to visit her, which despite being good soon became dangerous.

My Dad had narcolepsy and had fallen asleep at the wheel more than once. We could always tell when he was getting sleepy because he would whistle this atonal, offbeat song. It was so annoying. One weekend while we were going to visit Mom, Dad had almost fallen asleep when out of nowhere a tire from an eighteen-wheeler became dislodged and began to plow its way toward us. We began to brace for the impact of the tire that was traveling well over one hundred miles per hour when it suddenly turned and plowed its way to the side of the road. At this point, I realized that there was a higher presence around us. Dad was so shocked by the event that he stayed awake the rest of the trip.

Our trips to visit Mom were always a little sad, but it was also good to see Mom. I had to make sure she was okay. The school year came and went, and Mom got to come home on occasion, but Dad's religious decision was taking its toll on those of us always at home. We dealt with it daily and Mom knew, as Moms always do, there were some issues she would have to handle herself.

My life was not as seriously affected by the religious change as much as my brother's. His life would never be the same. Tyson had the one thing he loved the most taken away.

He was an all-star baseball player and won many state championships for the local area team, the Hawks. My dad, fully immersed in the Kingdom Hall, pulled my brother from baseball quoting, "Bad association spoils useful habits," whatever that was supposed to mean. From that point on, my brother was never the same. His one love in life was stripped from him. I don't think he ever forgave Dad for that. Mom, being Mom, knew we weren't happy, and from her hospital bed she became focused on changing that. On one of our many trips to visit her, she had managed to secretly plan a surprise birthday party for my seventh birthday. She instructed my Aunt Terri, her older sister, to arrange a party at Showbiz Pizza. She also enlisted the aid of her brothers to keep Dad occupied. This was by far my best birthday ever. One, because it was no longer allowed to happen, and two, Mom had planned it in spite of her illness and Dad's wishes. I gained a whole new respect for my Mom. I knew I would never forget it.

In July of 1987, despite all the things she'd done to make us feel special, Mom's disease had begun to worsen. She was put on bed rest and given six months to live. She called my brother and me in one at a time and said her tearful goodbye, but deep inside she knew she wouldn't give up. She kept a positive outlook on life, and in mid-December at the end of her six months, the doctors begged to care-flight Mom to a cancer specialist and she refused. She vowed that if by daybreak the next day she was not better, she would go. The night eased into the sunrise of the next day, and she indeed was better. I was so happy to see my Mom recovered that I was teary-eyed. When I say recovered, I mean completely and totally cured of all trace of cancer. The doctors were simply amazed because in a matter of twenty-four hours the cancer had somehow completely disappeared. Mom was so strong in her faith, and knew God was going to come through for her.

He did.

Since cancer was no longer an issue, my life resumed as close to normal as possible, remember, I was still a Witness. When Mom came home she immediately thanked my Granny. Granny and Mom looked so much alike that the family used to call her Lil' Jo since Granny's name was Josephine. Granny supported her during the cancer, and was always available to take her to and from

Dallas for all her treatments. I remember riding in Mom's car with Granny, she would just stare at us with a grimacing look through the rearview mirror. Granny was strong too, I guess it runs in the family. She raised her own kids and then offered to raise Aunt Button's son, Jake, so he would be in a more stable setting. Aunt Button is what one would call free-spirited, and I do mean "free." Aunt Button was mom's half-sister. She was the product of a man Granny married after she divorced Mom's dad. Aunt Button was of a milk chocolate complexion with short dark hair and a face full of baby fat and other signs of youth. She was a few inches shorter than mom.

Granny and Aunt Button were convinced Tyson and I were out to get Jake, so they would always keep one eye on us. Jake was spoiled, and he had asthma, which he used to his advantage. If he was in trouble or had done something wrong, he would complain about his wheezing and request the medication he called "slow bid." Oftentimes, Tyson and I wanted to get revenge on Jake for getting away with the things he did, but Granny always saved him. One time, we were playing outside as children do, when out of nowhere Jake decided he wanted to run me over with his tricycle. Obviously he had planned it, because he peddled as fast as he could from the edge of Granny's yard and ran over me. A piece of metal from the tricycle became lodged in my leg and let's just say the blood was flowing. Realizing that he might get in trouble, Jake fell to the ground and began his "skit", but by then I was hopping on one leg inside the house to show Aunt

Button the real deal. Aunt Button immediately grabbed a white towel from the linen closet and wrapped it around my leg. She didn't have a car and Granny was not home, so she had to call the neighbors to take me to the emergency room. This little incident finally helped the truth about Jake be known. Tyson and I had finally won some freedom although I was a casualty of this little war.

On the way to the hospital I could see this fatty white tissue with blood on it coming out of my leg. Once inside the hospital, the ER doctor had to put nine stitches in my leg. I remember every stitch because in an effort to stop the bleeding, he did not deaden the skin enough. When Mom arrived on the scene, I was in tears and she promised me that if I was a big boy she'd take me to McDonald's and get me my favorite, a Happy Meal. She knew that was all it would take, as every Mom does. Sure enough, she did just that—I got my happy meal in one of those orange pumpkin pails that McDonald's uses around Halloween time. With my leg all stitched up and the pain ceasing, I was able to return to the thing I loved most, school.

My teachers that year were Mrs. Jennings, my reading teacher, and Mrs. Holiday, my homeroom teacher. Homeroom was easy because I loved to read. That year, a new reading program called "Book It!" was introduced to my school. "Book It!" was a program that provided the incentive of a free personal pizza from Pizza Hut for every ten books read. To get a pizza, you'd have to either tell a story about one of the books or write a paragraph about it. At that time I was really interested in astronomy, so I was always at the library reading books by Isaac Asimov. I read books about all nine planets, the stars, and black holes. Yeah, I was a nerd, but I was also trying to get some pizza. Pizza is like McDonalds, the food that kids by far most enjoy. It was a sure win for me and my parents. I was always in the mood for pizza or Mickey D's. That year, I read over two hundred books and had several boxes of pizza. You do the math. Reading was my escape from the religious problems at home. Mrs. Jennings eventually got to the point where she would have two "Book It!" stickers ready for me every other Friday. That was a good year, but that summer Dad curbed my joy of reading when he made us start reading the Watchtower.

The Watchtower is the monthly publication of the subjects to be discussed during service. Dad would wake my brother and me up at six o'clock every Sunday morning to highlight and review the answers to the topics presented in that week's study. At home, Dad would pop my brother and me on the legs if we fell asleep during such readings. I thought Mom had a sour taste in fashion, but with Dad's taste all you could say was, "Oh, God," or in our case, "Oh, Jehovah!" Tyson escaped Dad's terrible fashion as he did with Mom, but me, I was dressed every Sunday in these tight-fitting black slacks, a white or off-white shirt, an awful brown tie with a lovely blue tie clip, and some black shoes with white socks. The outfits were, in a word, horrid. My brother and I were so sleepy from getting up so

23

early that we would often fall asleep during service. Tyson was able to get away with sleeping, but I was always startled by a pinch from Dad's meaty hand. To ensure that I would not get pinched, I studied Tyson's sleep tactics. He had his sleep posture and movements down to a science. He would take his right hand and place it above his eyes to make it appear as though he was really concentrating on the Watchtower, when in actuality he was asleep. Going to the Kingdom Hall was not all bad, because it was at the Hall I met my first friend. In the late summer of 1988 the Garnett family moved to our little town.

The Garnetts had two sons, one my age and another about a year younger than Tyson. I immediately became friends with their youngest son Aaron, aka AJ. Brian, AJ's older brother, became friends with Tyson. The Garnetts were the typical lower middle class white family. Brian had a severe heart condition, and thus was a bit spoiled by his parents. Most of the time if he wanted something, or if something didn't go his way, he would complain of a throbbing pain in his chest. It reminded me of Fred Sanford on Sanford and Son when he would complain of the "big one coming." Summer passed and it was time to return to school again. AJ, being the new kid at school, was put in the outcast category. He really did not have to worry, I was in the same category because I just didn't fit in with the other kids. AJ and I spent lots of time together. We spent nights at each other's houses and played a lot of Nintendo. In 1988, a Nintendo was the thing to have. Our favorite games were Zelda and Mario Brothers. Nintendo was my favorite pastime, but Mom and Dad would not allow me to play it on school nights for fear that it would spoil my education. Our teacher this year was Mrs. Green.

Mrs. Green taught us many things ranging from history to multiplication. I was always a smart child, but multiplication was determined to take me out. I recall making borderline grades in multiplication, because I could not grasp the concept behind it. Being an analytical child, in order to understand it, I had to analyze and determine the reason that multiplication worked the way it did. Other than the issues with multiplying, this year was exceptionally easy. When the school had holiday parties I was no longer the only student who had to leave. The Garnetts were also Jehovah's Witnesses, so AJ had to leave also. Before the Garnetts moved to Kittyhawk, I would always have to wait in the front office for a relative to come and pick me up. Now that AJ was here, we would go to his house and play video games while all the other kids stayed at school and celebrated. AJ lived across the street from school. Having a friend who could understand what I was going through made me feel better about my religion, because I no longer felt alienated. The school year passed rather quickly and before it was over, I had finally mastered multiplication. The summer of 1989 came and life was great. I had a friend and nothing was terribly wrong at home. Also, Mom had started taking classes to get her nursing license. Mom and Dad had their usual conflicts of interest over religion, which made for interesting dinner conversation.

Life continued at its regular pace until around mid-July, when Granny became very sick. Granny, knowing full well that she was sick, pushed her illness to the back burner to care of Jake and Mom. Mom was completely devastated when she discovered Granny had a malignant bleeding cancer. In 1987, Granny's doctor had diagnosed her illness, but because of a patient-doctor confidentiality agreement the family was not made aware. Over the years, Granny's cancer had become full-blown and there was really nothing that could be done to curb the disease. The cancer slowly ate away at Granny's existence, and I felt it eating away at Mom's.

Granny's cancer disseminated across her as a fire spreads through a dry grass field. I saw Mom becoming more emotional and stressed to the point where she was hospitalized. Some of the main contributors to her stress factor were school and Granny's illness. Mom's cancer did not destroy Granny, but her own cancer was determined to. Due to the type of cancer Granny had, there was a smell of rotting flesh in her bedroom. Granny, being the individual she was, tried her best to mask it, but such a pungent smell cannot be hidden. Granny continued on living until the fall of 1989, when her cancer progressed to an all-new high.

While Granny was battling cancer, life for me started anew. It was a brand new school year with new teachers. I was in the fourth grade at Preston Intermediate

School. To be totally honest, I had some excellent teachers, but I do not remember their names. AJ, my first cousin Tyrone, and I spent days, nights, and weekends playing Mario Brothers 3, Zelda 2, dodgeball, and hide-and-seek. My life was great, but there was a storm brewing on the horizon between Mom and Dad. My life couldn't have been any better, but Granny was slowly wasting away.

School was my only escape from the sorrow my Mom felt for Granny, which was complicated by the stress of Mom's schooling and the problems between my father and her. Mom and I had developed a very special bond during her cancer. It was, in a sense, spiritual in that I could feel her joy and sorrow. Right now I could sense all her pain and needed school to help keep me stable. This school year was most interesting. I faced several obstacles, and my world, that I had worked so hard to create, was entering a dark age.

First, my bus driver took it upon himself to introduce me to my first taste of real life. No, no, no, it's not what you're thinking, get your mind out the gutter. He was a shrewd little white man who was bitter because he was only a bus driver and no longer had the potential that we on the bus had, I guess. I had always known racial prejudices existed, but never had I experienced it up close and personal. One afternoon on our normal route home, the children, a little overexcited about the upcoming weekend, began talking and made a fair amount of noise. This was nothing out of the ordinary, the same groups were loud every Friday. Before I realized it, the bus driver had put the bus in park and began to walk toward the loudest group, a collection of black girls. He told them, "If you niggers don't be quiet, y'all are gonna be walking home!" I was completely astounded at the fact that he had just called those girls niggers. I immediately shrunk down in my seat and became very quiet. I had never heard someone call anyone of color a "nigger" in my presence. At each stop he made sure that he addressed anyone of color as a nigger before they exited the bus. At one stop a white boy got off the bus, and he addressed him as a "nigger lover" because he predominantly associated with the black children. Soon after he exited it was my turn to exit the bus, and because I had dropped my pencil it took me a little longer to reach the exit. As I approached the exit I heard, "Nigger, you better hurry!" I ran inside the house and began to cry in the family room. Only a few moments passed before I began to wipe the tears from my face. Shortly after, none other than my big brother appeared and asked why I was crying. I told him and immediately he grabbed my hand and walked me to my Aunt Erletta's, my Dad's older sister, because Mom and Dad were not home. Aunt Erletta was extremely smart, she was a nurse, but at times I thought she was a little too smart for her own good. She stood about five feet nine inches and had a light brown complexion. She had one quirky thing about her though, and that was her cough. It sounded like she was about to lose a lung, the only thing I could attribute it too was her smoking habit. I can honestly say that killed the interest in smoking for me.

I was still so shocked by the whole event that my brother had to tell my Aunt Erletta for me. After listening to the story she became infuriated, immediately jumped in her seafoam green Ford LTD, and sped up to school. She filed a complaint with the school principal, Mr. MacDowell. He assured my aunt that the situation would be rectified, but we all knew this was just to pacify us for the moment.

Later that day, Mom came home and was informed of the situation. Mom, being an assertive woman, took my aunt's original complaint a few steps further. She visited with all the parents of the children who rode the bus that day and obtained over fifty signatures of concerned and angry parents. With these signatures, she marched into the superintendent's office with a formal letter of complaint. She was assured that the issue would be rectified. Mom was invited to attend the next board meeting since the issue would be addressed. Mom and I attended the meeting that was held in the high school auditorium. After careful deliberation, the board members decided to relieve the driver from his bus responsibilities, but they still allowed him to teach his vocational courses. Mom accepted this as reasonable, even though I felt he should have been completely relieved of his duties pertaining to the school district.

The bus incident allowed me to see Mom become actively involved in something other than worrying about

Granny's health. Granny was dying and we all knew. We tried to focus on happier things, but it was a waste of time. It had been about two years since I had seen a hospital for personal reasons, but two months after the bus crisis, I was there again.

At school on my way from the library with my reading class, I was blown against a brick wall by a strong, gale force wind. I was a small person and was immediately knocked unconscious when my head hit the wall. Finally waking up, all I can recall is the heart and cerebral monitors of all different shapes, sizes, and styles. I remember there were the EEGs, the EKGs, and people moving busily around me. After scanning my brain several times it was concluded that I suffered a minor concussion. I sat in my hospital room with IVs running out my arms; I received mushy hospital food, balloons, and plenty of get well cards. I was released from my medical prison one week later. Home at last was the only thought I could let creep into my head, and life resumed to my level of normalcy. Due to life's circumstances, I began to submerge myself in school. Mom was having issues dealing with a dying mother, and Dad was busy trying to force a religion on his family that no one wanted to embrace. Tyson turned to his friends to escape life, and I was preparing to turn to mine when I was stopped abruptly. AJ's family moved away. AJ's father was dismissed for what was said to be adulterous reasons. This was a separation that I had wished would never happen. Life could not have been more difficult, my one and only friend had been stripped from me. My life, my happiness, my friendship, and my soul were crushed when AJ left. I was now left with a huge void in my heart with no one to help me fill it. I was alone in my world again.

In an attempt to cheer me up and adjust the mood in the house, we decided to go to Disney World. Shortly before the trip, Mom had finally completed her nurses program and received her nursing license. Granny was feeling a little better, so we all felt safe when we left our problems behind and attended the commencement ceremonies. In early August, we left at midnight on our voyage to Florida. The Mangol and Huntley families joined us, and all three families were members of the Kingdom Hall. I remember crossing over the seemingly endless dirty Mississippi River, stopping at a restroom in Georgia that smelled of urine and waste, and seeing the acres of orange trees outside of Orlando. Once at Disney World, I must admit I was awestruck and completely forgot about my worries. We went to Magic Kingdom and I met Mickey Mouse, Donald Duck, and just about every other character you would want to meet. Then we visited Epcot Center and MGM Studios to see the background effects of some movies like E.T. and Honey I Shrunk the Kids. For the finale, we visited Destine Beach.

For those who haven't been, I have to try and put into words what this place was like...the beach is like a glimpse as to what heaven might offer. There were emerald green and deep, sea-blue waters surrounded by white sand as far as the eye could see. We laughed and played in the sands as though this was our personal piece of heaven; this trip allowed our minds to be liberated from the troubles that plagued each of our lives. We spent the whole day there and when we began to leave this celestial place the clouds that surrounded my life overshadowed my happiness. When we returned, Mom suffered her first separation.

In October of 1990, Granny's cancer had finally destroyed her.

CHAPTER THREE

LOOK TO THE HILLS...

In the waiting room, the doctors approached our family and officially announced that Granny was dead. I immediately saw Mom's face dismantle. A cloud of sorrow surrounded my family. We didn't have to do much in final preparation for the funeral because Granny had already completed most things. Granny had written her funeral program, and divided her assets amongst her nine surviving children. She was not by any means wealthy, but what she left behind was worth more than any platinum, gold, or silver. Granny imparted knowledge and initiative to her children to go, to do, and never give up. The guidance and direction she gave to Mom changed my life. Mom was able to instill within me those same values. She never allowed me to settle for silver when I had gold potential. During the funeral, Mom's life was changed.

Out of all nine children, Mom took it the worst. Mom and Granny had an extremely special bond that had been strengthened during Mom's sickness, but was silenced quickly with Granny's death. She was the glue that held the family together, but now with her gone, one might wonder who could keep this divided family together. In the midst of the funeral, the torch was seemingly passed from Granny's soul to Mom's soul. Mom became the glue. During the middle of the ceremony, Aunt Button, now twenty-one, burst through the doors of Saints Rising Baptist Church to beg for Granny's forgiveness. Aunt Button was sorry for not being the daughter she should have been, for not being a mother figure in Jake's life, and for just being a poor example of the family. I guess when one accepts the fact that they have been too negligent, the repercussions can be devastating. Granny was and is surely missed, but now with someone to take over her position, Granny could rest in peace.

After the funeral, the whole family went through a change, each in our own way. Mom was the most affected by Granny's passing, but apparently she wasn't going to have long to focus on mourning. Whispers were circling all around town concerning Mom and Dad. Mom, being a very church-oriented individual, turned the other cheek. Mom was steadfast and had patience when she dealt with small town people and their comments. In the months following the funeral, the arguments over respect or lack thereof escalated. It never failed that in an argument I would hear, "You just don't respect me, do you?!"

In an effort to hide his shortcomings, Dad suddenly stopped going to the Kingdom Hall. He insisted that Tyson and I continue instead, but we no longer had reason to attend. AJ was gone, so I did not have a drive to go, and as for Tyson, he never really liked going, so this was right up his alley. We stopped going altogether about January of 1991. Living in a house where there is a problem between your parents and you are left in the dark about it is not a great feeling. Tyson knew more about the problem than I did because all I heard were the arguments. Tyson had heard it from all his friends. I did not want to see the issues that plagued my household, so again I turned to school for escape.

For every curse word or tear that was shed, I made one point higher on every test and increased my class grade. Math, science, and English became my mother, father, and my brother. Dad was never active in my academic career so he did not really notice a change. Mom noticed, but she was too wrapped up in her own problems to say or do anything about my change. Tyson started staying out late and sometimes not even coming home. So he didn't notice any change within me either. Tyson was now in the height of his teenage years. He was the cute, light-skinned guy with a "box" haircut that dressed in all the latest urban fashions. What can I say, he deserved all the attention he got from the ladies. I guess like father, like son. In the spring of 1991, Tyson turned to alcohol as a fix for his problems. He was only fifteen. Tyson's grades were always pretty fair, but suddenly they dropped due to his extra-curricular activities. Dad was still trying to cover his tracks behind the rumors floating through town. He tried to befriend Tyson by sponsoring his alcohol habit. He would purchase Tyson any type of alcohol he wanted. He took it a step further when he bought Mom a new car.

It was obvious to both Mom and me that something was "motivating" Dad to be so generous. Was he trying to mask the problems in the house? Was he the cause? Anyways this behavior wasn't groundbreaking or anything special because whenever Dad fell short at fatherhood or being a good husband he bought his way out. Dad felt that by buying Tyson liquor and Mom a new car he would earn their respect back. Dad had lost Tyson's respect long ago when he pulled Tyson from baseball. I guess, in a sense, he was trying to bribe his oldest son.

The new car did not patch up his relationship with Mom either. It only made things worse. Mom was driving a 1990 Lincoln Town Car then, becoming more subjected to people's comments and living in a household that she really did not desire to deal with. Tyson, on the other hand, was not even dealing with the situations at home; he was now a late-night alcoholic hoodlum. Now, if you want to call names, he whole-heartedly fulfilled the stereotype of what and how being a "nigga" is described. He forgot about his studies and learned lessons in how to get over in life. Just as Dad was trying to pacify Tyson, their relationship went down the hole. One beautiful spring morning in 1991 turned violent.

Dad saw Tyson hanging out on the corner, and demanded that he come home. This did not settle too well with Tyson, because he questioned why Dad would now try to express his authority when he had not been doing it in the past. Dad and Tyson exchanged words that night, but that following morning was when the shit hit the fan. Tyson decided to finally bring himself home, and Dad was waiting on the sofa by the front door for him. Instantly, I was awakened to the sound of cursing and fighting. As I exited my room, I walked toward the sound of the commotion to discover Dad and Tyson fighting. Mom was trying to break up the fight, but she wasn't having much success. The fight waged on until I made a very critical decision. During the course of the fight I ran to my room and began to cry. I could not deal with this problem so I packed my things to leave. I packed enough socks, underwear, and clothes to last me at least a week. On my way out the door, Mom noticed me, crying with bags in hand, and begged for them to stop. They stopped, but the aftermath was horrid. A new wooden bedroom suite was now destroyed, and I was forever damaged.

With the physical altercation over, I now had to endure a man and a child shouting verbal obscenities throughout the house. Dad said that Tyson was no longer his son, and Tyson stated that Dad was not his father. Dad placed me on a pedestal, and proclaimed that I was his one and only son. Dad basically did this to anger Tyson. By doing so, this distanced Tyson and me more than we already were. Plus, their father and son relationship was now completely destroyed.

That same night, Mom, trying to resolve this family crisis, decided on another separation. Out of fear for Tyson's life, Mom decided to remove him from such a volatile situation. She called Dad's younger brother and sister-in-law, Vincent and Eloise, and arranged for Tyson to go live with them. I didn't know much about Uncle Vincent and Aunt Eloise. I knew they were extremely educated and were a well-established urban black family. Uncle Vincent only came down every once in a while from the big city so I didn't get to know much about him. He was a handsome man of a lighter complexion, muscle-toned, with green eyes, and Aunt Eloise, with her stern face, was quite the head-turner herself. This would have explained how she and my uncle got married. Tyson was to reside with them until his high school career was completed. He was a sophomore. That night, Tyson packed all his belongings and Mom drove him to his new home in Worthwood. Mom felt deep within her heart that if she didn't get Tyson out it would be the death of him. Tyson, on the other hand, could not comprehend why Mom opted to do this, so it put a strain on their relationship. Tyson wanted us all to leave, not just him. Mom could not leave yet because there was some unfinished business. She did not feel my life was in direct danger, so she allowed me to stay.

After we arrived in Worthwood, Mom left her oldest son in the care of my aunt and uncle. Uncle Vincent and Aunt Eloise asked Mom to allow me to stay as well, but Mom had already made the decision for me to stay with her. As we pulled out of the driveway a tear ran down my cheek. I was now faced with having a "spirit" brother. The return trip home was silent and sad. Neither Mom nor I spoke the one hundred eighty miles back to Kittyhawk. I felt the hurt Mom was experiencing and I saw it in her eyes. I only hoped that life would get better now.

After we arrived in Kittyhawk, we entered the house and went into our rooms and closed the doors. I do not know what went on behind her wooden door, but I could imagine. Behind my door sat a sad, teary-eyed boy who silently watched television. That had to be the hardest night ever. I had to come to terms with my estranged brother. I cried myself to sleep, and the next morning, I awoke to an argument between Mom and Dad over her decision. Dad was angry because Mom had not consulted him in this matter concerning Tyson. My dad could not understand why she did it, but I thought to myself what mother would not have done the same thing if their child was in danger. The arguments over this went on for several days until finally they stopped. I figured that the idea of Tyson leaving had finally settled in with him. He realized that Tyson was going to complete his high school career in Worthwood, and that there was nothing that could be done about it. When life had resumed to a close proximity of what we knew as normal, the arguments over the whispers started again.

It was the fall of 1991, and I was in the sixth grade. I had finally arrived at Wilson Junior High School. I was always academically inclined, so my peers viewed me as a nerd. I was not a physical person, so physical education (PE) had a time with me. I excelled in my studies, but when it came to running and exercising, I failed miserably. I did just enough in PE to get by and keep from looking like a total nerd. I had now entered that awkward stage in my life where my physical features were going through the change. Some features that did not change were my chubby cheeks, chunky, thick legs, and high booty. I had a lot of book sense, but I had never mastered the art of common sense. Simple tasks like determining "true" versus "false" people presented a problem for me. I was so naïve that even the dumbest individual could talk a good game and lure me in. I wore glasses and acted eccentric, so girls just loved taking advantage of me, and I, oblivious to the truth, went right along for the ride.

My first major "ride" was Traci. Traci was that girl in school who just seemed out of reach to any and every one. Traci was taller than me, with skin that was kissed with chocolate and long black hair. She was it, with those perfect eyes, and lips. I was hooked. Like most, I worshipped the ground she walked on. I had issues with the way I looked, "some of y'all understand," so when she spoke to me I felt privileged. After hanging out for a few weeks, we became boyfriend and girlfriend. I was so happy to have a girlfriend that my parents' issues ceased to

40

bother me. I was so gullible that I quickly fell in love with Traci. She was so nice and always wrote these romantic letters that I kept in my gray treasure vault.

A few weekends prior to my getting a girlfriend, Dad and Mom got into an argument about him and some other woman. The woman had said something to Dad. This was all I could gather from the argument. Mom decided to take us to Dana's house in Longhandle, Texas. Dana was my godmother who had also experienced some of the same things that plagued my parents' marriage. Dana had always been pretty, and had a sultry voice that made you want to listen to her. She always dressed in dark clothes and wore sunglasses so I just knew she was cool back in the day, but boy, was I fooled. Eavesdropping on a conversation between her and Mom I learned, every time she had her shades on she was hiding the bruises and marks left by her husband. She was someone that Mom could relate to. Dana had separated from her husband, so she knew full well what preceded her separation and could recognize the symptoms. Mom just told me that this was a vacation, but I knew there must have been more to the story. I realized very quickly that this was an escape for Mom. She had begun to look toward the hills for help. While in Longhandle, Mom was able to regain some peace of mind and vent to Dana. I chose not to see what issues really plagued the household, so this weekend was a bit unnecessary for me. I played with my god-sister, Shon, and watched movies all weekend. On the final day of our trip, Shon gave me a gray treasure vault, so I could store my secrets and keep my fears hidden. It had a combination lock that made it difficult for people to pry into my personal business. When we returned home, Dad was apologetic to Mom, and he even had a surprise for her.

While we were away, the neighbors across the street had cooked up a big pot of catfish head stew. Dad took it upon himself to save a portion for Mom. When Mom found out what type of stew it was, she refused to eat it. Dad got so upset over this he threw it against the bathroom wall. Mom, determined not to clean it up, allowed it to sit and spoil for several weeks until the smell became unbearable. She eventually cleaned it up, but these events did not really bother me because I had Traci. I revered Traci so much that I would walk a couple of steps behind her in school or anywhere if we were together. My emotions had me in a complete state of confusion and bewilderment. With my allowance, I bought Traci teddy bears, flowers, and cards for holidays and her birthday. My sixth-grade year passed by very quickly, but the one major memory of this year, besides Traci, was my sixth grade science class's trip to Disney World. To go on the summer trip, each person was required to pay six hundred dollars. I wanted to go really bad, so Dad paid my way. I enjoyed my family trip there, so I could only imagine what being in a group full of my peers was going to be like. Mom was not going to allow me to go that far away from home without her, so she volunteered to be a chaperone. Even though she was a chaperone, she still had to pay the fees. The trip there was terrible. The bus seats were crammed together and some of the students had developed odor problems. When I felt extremely crammed and smelled too many feet and armpits, I thought of Traci, and everything was okay. Once we arrived, I was finally able to breathe freely again and stretch out. I rushed off the bus. The hotel stay was okay. I had to room with two familiar school classmates. I went to Magic Kingdom, Epcot Center, Universal Studios, and Cocoa Beach. None of the four places were fun at all. We walked from 8 a.m. to 11 p.m. every day. In Magic Kingdom, I got lost and no teachers or chaperones would help me find my group again as we were told not to wander away from our groups. I guess the chaperones felt since I wandered off, I should be responsible for locating my group again. Surely, they wouldn't be thinking that I was not their problem or their kid. At Epcot Center, I got split up from my group and was left to wander for hours until my mom found me. Universal Studios was not as bad, we just had to walk forever with no rest stops in the humid weather. Cocoa Beach was the worst of them all, because the beach was nothing like Destine Beach. It had brown sand, dirty, brownish-gray water, and a high jellyfish population. Needless to say, if I had wanted to go swimming, I couldn't have. Once the trip was over, Mom and I vowed never to take a school-sponsored trip of that magnitude again.

For me, this trip never compared to the family vacation, because even for the twelve hundred plus dollars spent between Mom and me, it was awful. When we got back to Kittyhawk, I rushed off the bus and went to see

Traci. Traci seemed so happy to see me back, and I was definitely happy to see her. The summer passed very quickly after that awful trip, but at the beginning of my seventh-grade year, my life completely fell apart.

First, my home life was sinking fast. Mom and Dad no longer communicated, they just argued. Mom and I shed several tears; I personally couldn't handle all the drama. Secondly, Traci was no longer in my life. Traci had used my kind heart and gullible personality to her own advantage. In the midst of spending my allowance on flowers, candy, and stuffed animals she had found a new love interest. I had always known that Traci was my superior, but I really felt she loved me as much as I loved her. I was crushed when I discovered she found comfort in talking to an older relative of mine. Her new interest was Tony, my older cousin. Tony was in high school and at that time, Traci felt he could do more for her than a little nerdy, naïve seventh grader. I had never kissed or touched her with any sexual intentions, so she left me. I was too book smart to have any common sense about intimacy in a relationship. To be completely honest, I didn't know what to do! Traci knew about those intimate things, and at this time in her life I am sure she felt I could not provide them for her. I loved Traci with every ounce of my being, but it was not enough for her. I didn't believe our relationship was over until one hot September day at school.

After lunch, all the seventh graders would go

outside to an open track field and socialize. I had always avoided this place, because I could never relate to the other kids, but I was determined that day to confront Traci for leaving me. I marched out to the field and asked Traci, with a stern look, why she did it. She told me things I never wanted to hear her say. She called me a nerd, an ugly, non-athletic boy, and told me that she never loved or even liked me, she just tolerated my company. I wasn't athletic because I didn't play football like the rest of the boys my age. I could not change being a nerd, because I was naturally smart, and learning came easy to me. Her words cut deep; I can't even put it into words, all I know is I was devastated. Every word cut deeper and deeper until finally I could not bear it anymore. I turned away with sadness, despair, and anger forming tear streams down my face. As I walked away she and her friends said other things, but I didn't hear them; the damage was complete. My heart hardened. I was determined never to allow my heart to be hurt again, so I killed my emotions.

I was frozen.

On the home front, Mom and Dad no longer slept in the same bedroom, and if they were in any room for an extended period of time an argument developed. Mom's patience and endurance had worn thin. One fall afternoon, I witnessed a verbal argument of a magnitude that I had never seen before. All I could gather from the argument was that Dad had done something terrible, and Mom was extremely upset, crying while she washed the dishes. Dad continued to argue when Mom snapped. She started throwing dishes like Frisbees at Dad. Mom broke almost every cup, plate, and glass in the house before she regained sanity and stopped. With Mom still in the kitchen and me in my bedroom trying to pretend I couldn't hear the commotion, Dad came into my room and told me that he would be leaving for a while. I started to cry and he told me that he would always love me and to always protect Mom. He left the house with bags in hand and moved to Aunt Erletta's house.

Aunt Erletta only lived a few blocks away, so it wasn't like he was leaving town. I was okay with him moving down the street, as long as Mom could deal with it. That night, Mom came to me and revealed what I had been so blind to all along. She told me the reason Dad had to leave and why they argued so much.

Dad had committed multiple acts of adultery against Mom. The townspeople had been talking about it since our family vacation to Disney World in 1990. Mom told me how our neighbor across the street would walk through her yard without a bra on to tease Dad and aggravate her, how he had slept with the daughter of a fellow church member, and how he had slept with one of Tyson's ex-classmates. This explained why Tyson could never seem to regain respect for Dad, and why they had such a strange relationship. Mom suffered the most, mainly because she knew of these things, but she was determined to try to keep her marriage together. Mom was able to deal with all the other women Dad had slept with but one. She could never forgive him for this act. She was a thorn in Mom's side and had a past that linked the two together.

The one woman who Mom could never forgive Dad for sleeping with was her sister. The revelation of this act leveled me and made me sick to my stomach. Sitting there frozen in disbelief I finally understood why he had to go.

The fact that he had hurt Mom the way he did drove me to break all emotional ties with him. Mom tried to continue life without Dad, but deep down she still loved him in spite of it all. Mom allowed Dad to come back into our lives three weeks later because Dad had promised to do right by her and by his family. Mom knew what was down the road, but she felt deep within that things would get better. Mom was determined not to let her marriage fail. Both Mom and I knew that it was over, but she would not, and could not, let go.

CHAPTER FOUR

JUDGE NOT...

What happens when the sun shines through a magnifying glass onto a leaf? It burns. It burns as the ties that bind a family together do when hearts have been broken. Mom allowed Dad to come back and attempt to patch the holes in their marriage and make all prior wrongs right. I had already decided that he didn't belong with us anymore. I could never forgive him for verbally and emotionally abusing us.

Dad immediately came back with a new zest for life. He tried to be the family man that we wanted, but was it really what he wanted? My emotions were dead, although Dad and Mom appeared to be getting along. Had Dad really changed? He started coming home on time and

48

paying attention to some of the things I did. Three weeks went by, and everything seemed better until the arguments started back up. As I lay asleep in my bed, I was awakened to sounds of yelling and crying. I had grown accustomed to not hearing any arguments by now, so this was a bit of a surprise. As I listened to the shouting, I learned that Mom had found some unknown phone numbers, condoms, and some type of STD kit in Dad's personal things. The leaf had begun to incinerate.

I eventually got back to sleep, and the next day things appeared to be more settled. I stayed in the house all the time because of my reclusive nature. Let's tally this up so far. Granny, AJ, Traci, and Tyson had all left my life in some way. Dad might as well have left, so I figured why bother venturing out. Besides, within me, there were some changes happening that I couldn't address because of the turmoil at home. My opinion of girls had changed since Traci, and I felt I could never trust another woman with my heart. This lack of trust introduced me to feelings I had long been covering up, a new spin on life. I started to find comfort in myself more than others did. I was a growing boy with sexual interests, and I did not have the know-how to go about satisfying them. I felt that I was too ugly to approach anyone, so I learned methods of self-pleasure. You know exactly what I mean. I continued to please myself until eventually it was overwhelming. I was obsessive-compulsive about this newfound pleasure. I had to have it all the time, at school, at home, at the park, or wherever the need came. I know what y'all are thinking, he's a little freaky, right? I was, I must admit, but I needed it. Any parents out there who have sons twelve and older might not know they're doing it, but trust me, they all do—but probably not as much as I did.

My seventh-grade year was more of a challenge. I was an office aide, and when I made rounds to pick up the attendance sheets I would stop at the bathroom by the eighth-grade classrooms and take care of business. This was not only my way to relieve sexual frustration, but an escape from the tension at home, and it became a daily routine. The arguments at home between Mom and Dad continued as if part of their daily routine, and I was left to learn more and more about "nature."

I came home from school, as usual, ready for some "self loving", only to find Mom crying and all our things by the front door. Mom had packed everything because she was tired. She called her cousin Janice to come and pick us up. She just couldn't take it anymore. Thank God, I thought, but Dad was so arrogant. He boasted proudly that he'd be there when Mom decided to crawl back, and that she'd never make it without him. It was almost as if he were predicting our failure. By the time Janice arrived, Dad had given Mom a two-week ultimatum to come back. Dad was either extremely certain that Mom would buckle in two weeks, or he was finally realizing that he was about to lose the most important people in his life, his family.

As we rode across town, I was silent as Janice

consoled Mom. Mom had made arrangements for us to reside with her father, Leroy. Granddaddy lived in a small, white, old house in the middle of nowhere. Granddaddy was a sweet, older man who had a love for dominoes and his daughter. He was a good cook; I mean, he could really throw down in the kitchen. Back when Dad was still a Jehovah's Witness, the entire family would meet over his house and eat homemade biscuits and chicken wings with gravy. Wings and biscuits, if you don't know, are great for breakfast. When we arrived at the house, I wished to be somewhere else. I had been raised in fairly well-to-do conditions, and this was a significant understatement to my character. This house had critters of all shapes, sizes, and colors crawling around. I wasn't happy by any means, but if Mom had peace of mind here, then so be it. I only slept there at night because I had to. At least Mom was there to protect me from the bugs. Any other time of day, I could be found with my Dad's younger sister, Alberta, her husband, Preston, and their son, Tyrone. Aunt Alberta was a character; she was what some might call eccentric. She was small in stature with a big heart, and a curl atop her head. She was and is the only woman I know of that can wear a curl and make it dynamite.

Many of the things that had transpired in our household were unknown outside the house. So Aunt Alberta being Aunt Alberta and not in the know made me feel welcome, loved, and helped me to temporarily put my problems away. Aunt Alberta had a smile and charisma about life that could brighten any melancholy atmosphere.

Preston and Alberta were very spiritual people, and honestly happy. I just couldn't understand how they could be so happy about life. I guess God made their life and home happy, but at the time he wasn't working for Mom and me so I camped out at their house as often as possible. I was drawn to the peace and joy I felt when I stayed at their house. I loved the fact that I never had to hear Uncle Preston and Aunt Alberta argue or fight. I could just enjoy being young, plus I loved spending time with my cousin, Tyrone.

Tyrone was Aunt Alberta's child from a previous marriage. He was younger, but felt he could do anything better than me. Tyrone and I were complete opposites. I was used to being with myself and Tyrone was not. Our two personalities collided a lot. When he wanted to run, play, and climb trees, I just wanted to sit in the house and play video games. I didn't see the point in going outside and getting all dirty and sweaty. Was it even safe out there? Why not just stay in the house and eat? At least I would be full and safe.

Long before Tyrone, I had retired my thoughts about sporty things and most physical activities for that matter, growing up with Deuce and Foxy was far too exhausting to exert extra energy elsewhere. When Aunt Alberta would make me go play I would always run out of breath and have to take frequent rest breaks. Didn't she know? I wasn't into all that. I was truly as non-physical as they came. Tyrone and his friends would tease me often, because I was chunky and non-athletic. Who cared, I was content in my own little world. Play, indeed—all those childish things were beneath me. You want to play? Come into my domain and play some video games. They used to tell me that my hands would turn into joysticks someday. I just didn't fit in with those other kids.

Back at home, Mom was busy trying to piece our lives back together. She wanted me to have some semblance of religion in my life, so she would send me to church with Uncle Preston and Aunt Alberta. I really didn't want to go because I had grown quite accustomed to sleeping in on Sundays, but Mom wanted me in church, so to church I went. I can remember the first time I stepped into a church.

Aunt Alberta and Uncle Preston went to First Church of the Living Lord's Gospel in a small neighborhood community called Raven's Nest. It was so loud in this church. My ears were ringing the whole service. I wasn't used to such noise. When I was a Witness against my will, we didn't make loud noises in the Kingdom Hall. I was startled to see people clapping, shouting, and running up and down the aisles. I actually thought it was a comedy show just for me. Aunt Alberta told me not to laugh at them because they had "caught the spirit." I didn't know what this "spirit" was, but I knew that if it made me stand up and dance and then pass out, I didn't want it. After that day, I never wanted to go back. Uncle Preston and Aunt Alberta would talk to me about the goodness of God, but I wasn't trying to hear that. I was angry at the world and God for my home being destroyed. I could no longer say "my parents," I could only say "my parent." Mom was busy working and planning so I was left to myself. Mom had started making several trips to Dallas to visit her brothers and sisters.

Mom had decided, at the advice of her older brother Bernard, to move to Dallas. They had planned for us to move the summer of my seventh-grade year. Mom had grown tired. She needed and desired a new beginning. She was tired of others scrutinizing her every move and judging the decisions she made. It was an exodus in her life, especially since the divorce was final. Mom had no reason to stay. She didn't have a husband or a mother anymore, so the only tie she had left was Dad's child support check. Dad had gotten out almost scot-free. He didn't have to pay more than five hundred dollars a month for two children, and he was hardly ever on time with the money. Dad felt that this was fair and that this was all he should have to pay. I felt otherwise. Based on income alone, he should have been required to pay five hundred dollars per child, at least. I guess this is what happens when both people involved in the divorce use the same lawyer. One person always gets the short end of the stick. Mom just happened to get that end. She would have to work much harder and longer to cover both our expenses. In spite of it all, she pulled through, as moms always do.

Mom didn't know quite how to break the news to

me, but one night she finally got around to it. We were riding around in her tan '89 Chrysler that she had purchased on one of her trips to Dallas when she just broke down and told me we were moving. I was in complete awe. I didn't know what to say, how to act, or what to do. All I knew was that everything I had been taught from childhood on was about to change. Somewhere deep inside I knew this had to be good since all I knew was bad, but still, this was too big an event for me to deal with.

"Going through the motions" is the best way to describe the remainder of the year. I was faced with the fact of leaving, and I didn't have a choice. I was angry with Mom for not talking to me before she made the decision. This decision not only would affect her, but it would affect me. I felt she was being selfish. I had already dealt with her marriage problems, and now this! Even though Dad had done many things wrong, he was still Dad and now he wouldn't be as easy to access. My family had no idea how deeply hurt and uprooted I felt. The only reason I was able to cope was because of the time I spent in Aunt Alberta and Uncle Preston's home.

On the last day of seventh grade, I finally realized it was all over. I said my good-byes to all of my peers, since I never really had any real friends. I smiled, but deep down I hurt like hell. Moreover, I was terrified of a big city like Dallas. I was remembering the trips to Dallas to visit Mom at Granville C. Morton Hospital, and I just didn't like it. The environment was more dangerous than that in Kittyhawk. I heard the horror stories of the children carrying guns and knives to school, was this Mom's idea of a better opportunity? So many things plagued my mind concerning the big move. I did what I did best, and went inside myself to deal with everything. The introverted child Tyrone had tried so hard to convert had a relapse on the cusp of my thirteenth birthday.

Summertime came along and with it my thirteenth birthday. Unlike most, this birthday was extremely depressing. As usual, I didn't have a party, nor have friends over. Mom and Dad just wished me a happy birthday as their schedules allowed over the course of the day. Dad had become more lenient on birthdays since he was no longer a member of the Kingdom Hall, and especially since he had a new interest in his life. Dad had acquired a new girlfriend since the divorce, Patricia. I called her Pat though, since Patricia sounded too old for her.

Pat was significantly younger than my father and had three children. She was twenty-three and was closer to my age than she was to Dad's, so we instantly formed a tight bond. June passed, and in July we moved from Kittyhawk to Garland, Texas, a suburb of Dallas.

Since we didn't have a place of our own, we stayed with my Mom's brother Bernard Blumfield and his family. Uncle Bernard, Aunt Sherry, Brian, and Shonica were very kind for allowing us to reside with them. I know y'all must be waiting for the dirt on these folks, but I'm not telling…that's all there is to say about that! Uncle Bernard was a very machismo, cocky, and arrogant man. I remember from time to time he and his family would come to Kittyhawk and share their big city ideas with us country folk. Just looking at him I could tell he was a talker and a playboy back in his day, but my, my, what a wife and kids will do to you. Aunt Sherry, on the other hand, was an educated, subservient woman. She stayed her place when it came to her husband. I wanted to look Uncle Bernard in the eye sometimes and tell him to shut up, but I never did. Brian was walking in his father's steps, already a cocky, self-assured tack at a young age. Shonica, what couldn't be said about her, she was a solid, short and sassy. I could tell she drove the boys wild with that caramel complexion, I guess that's why she was pregnant. Mom didn't have a job yet, so every day she went on interviews until she was hired at Bayview Hospital. Shonica was pregnant, so she babysat Brian and me. All we ever did was play video games so her job was never hard. Aunt Sherry and Uncle Bernard reminded me of Aunt Alberta and Uncle Preston because they always talked about God. Their home was very different from Aunt Alberta and Uncle Preston's because there were arguments and discussions all the time. During the summer it was decided that I would attend Acorn Middle School with Brian. Brian was in the sixth grade and I was in the eighth grade, but Uncle Bernard and Aunt Sherry noticed that wasn't the only difference between Brian and me.

Since I had spent the majority of my childhood

years around my mother, I had feminine tendencies. I wasn't like the other boys my age, I guess. Brian and I played and we would oftentimes do immature things to one another. Things like pulling each other's pants down and giving each other wedgies. Uncle Bernard and Aunt Sherry had a meeting about these activities one day while Mom was at work. I was asleep in our bedroom when I woke up to the sound of Uncle Bernard's voice. I didn't move, I just listened from the bed to the discussion. They were talking about me. Uncle Bernard said to Brian, "You can play with your cousin, but because he's gay, keep your distance." I thought to myself, am I gay? What is gay? What does it feel like, that gay thing? Everything I had heard about gay up until this point was bad. Was I a bad kid? This hurt, because I would have never thought my family could say such things about me. My brain refused to accept gay. I softly grumbled, "I'm not gay!", but their words haunted me.

The new school year started and I excelled, as I always do in adverse conditions, in all my classes except one. Mrs. Greer taught my algebra class. I made borderline grades in algebra. It was too complex for me to understand. I just couldn't grasp the concept behind it. You remember how multiplication messed my life up. Well, this subject just didn't make sense, and she taught it on a level far above the class. She expected us to learn it simply from lectures and tests. I struggled through algebra, but this wasn't nearly as bad as what I experienced when dealing with my peers. I just didn't fit in with those other kids, as usual.

The "gay" issue came up again and again. I didn't dress like everyone else. I liked colors. All my clothes were purples, yellows, greens, and reds. I didn't wear blue denim jeans, and I didn't play sports. Because I liked colors and I didn't like sports I was labeled as "gay." I tried not to let it bother me, but it did. I can remember taking hot showers at night, sitting in the tub basin allowing the water to wash my tears away. I couldn't deal with it. My family agreed with my peers. I didn't feel gay, but who was I to say anything. Mom was my knight in shining armor. She stood in my defense. She didn't believe I was gay, nor did she accept them labeling me. I fed off her strength. She gave me words of encouragement, and everyone else's words began to roll off my back. The words became as whispers in the wind.

During the holidays, Dad would pick me up and take me back to the house. While with Dad I was plucked for information, and I was fed negative information about my mom. One time we were entering Winifred, TX when Dad turned to me and asked, "How is life in Garland?" I responded, "It's okay." Dad then asked, "Are you able to buy the things you want to buy?" I said no. He kept prying for more information, until I broke down and told him that I hated living in Garland, and I wished I could come back home. That's all he needed to hear. He immediately twisted my words to say that I was living in poverty, and that Mom was too proud to admit failure. Dad requested this information every time I came to visit, and Mom wanted the same when I came back home. I was put in a "pick your favorite parent" battle. I felt as though I was required to give them this information in order to receive the love and attention I so desperately craved. I continued to be the informant for both parents until I separated myself from Dad. My dad, busy trying to relive his parenting years with a new woman and other kids, devastated me. Dad, now completely separated from the Kingdom Hall, allowed the new kids to celebrate birthdays and Christmas. This hurt me deeply because all I ever wanted was to celebrate one Christmas where I was given gifts like the other kids. This didn't seem to bother Dad, but it was enough to sear the bond that was developing between us. I can remember thinking, Why me? Why can't Dad love me the same way he loves those other kids? He seemed to believe that since he paid child support that was all he needed to do. Mom couldn't see my hurt, all she could see was my rebellion. I rebelled against her because I wanted to vent the anger and pain that Dad had caused, but I couldn't. I wanted him to give me the love I deserved. I was his son, unlike those other kids.

After coming back from a visitation with him I would often say hurtful things to Mom like, "You'll never be able to take care of me like Dad," "You should've never left him," and "I wish you'd just give up and go back to him." I just said those things out of hurt and disgust. I knew the words hurt, because I could sometimes hear Mom talking with the pastor of her church, and I could see the dried tears on her face. Mom walked a lonely path at this time except for the two things that meant most to her. One was her father, Leroy, and the other was God. Mom had grown closer to both since Granny's death. She had formed a very strong bond with Granddad during the time when she decided to leave Dad. Mom would make frequent trips back home to see Granddaddy, because he had started to complain of some health problems. Mom went down there to take him to the doctor and to care for him. She was able to do so, because since moving to Dallas we were finally somewhat stable.

Mom was now working full-time for Medical Complex of Dallas, and we lived away from Uncle Bernard and his family. We lived in Cinnamon Place, and for once we had peace of mind. Mom didn't have to worry about them interfering in her affairs, and I didn't have to worry about their condescending comments. A month or so before we moved, the tensions, the attitudes, and the stress had increased to extreme levels. Mom was constantly exchanging words with Uncle Bernard and Aunt Sherry, and I had altercations with their children. I had to deal with derogatory comments from Brian like "fag" and "gay boy," and put up with Shonica's attitude. This was only the beginning.

One fall day, as I was washing dishes, Shonica was sitting on the sofa being her irritable pregnant self and Brian was cleaning the living room when an argument developed. Shonica looked at me and said, "You better

61

hurry up and finish those dishes!" and I responded, "I'll finish them when I finish."

"Don't test me boy, and you better listen to me."

"You are not my mother or my father, so until you become one or the other, then you have no say."

After I said this Shonica sprang up from the couch and pushed all of the glasses and plates on the counter toward me. Every dish hit the ground, not only creating a huge mess, but making this horrific crash sound. Shonica, now hyped about the situation, said, "I told you not to test me!" and I responded, "Whatever, girl don't go there with me." Shonica continued to say things, but I just ignored her, but I could hear Brian reiterating over and over, "Ooooooooh, y'all gonna get it when Momma and Daddy come home." I swept up the plates and glasses and put them in the trash. I felt deep down that there was more to it than this. When Aunt Sherry came home she made all three of us line up in living room and get licks. I didn't cry. I was still angry with Shonica. It was funny to see Shonica dance around and proclaim that she shouldn't get hit with the belt because she was pregnant. For each of her licks she said, "Momma, oh God!" When Mom came home it was decided that we needed to start making preparations to leave. We moved in mid December. Mom had found us a two-bedroom apartment in Cinnamon Place.

CHAPTER 5

BLESSED BE THE MAN...

All things are possible to him that believeth…

In the months following our escape from the Blumfield household, life finally started to feel like life again. I had started my emotional and physical transition from a little country boy to a young, urbanized teenager. I left what I like to call the Acorn Saga in my past. Mom and I began to grow together as a mother and son should. It was no longer Mom and me against one another, it was more like a bond of love and strength under God. God had become the center of both our lives.

I began to attend church on a regular basis. Summertime came, and life was good. At fourteen, I was quite ready to join the working world. Not one

63

company would give me job, because of my age. I was disheartened a little because I wanted so much to lessen the load on Mom's shoulders. I realized for the first time that Mom was a struggling single parent. She worked full-time at Medical Complex, but funds had to be stretched to pay every bill. At times, some things were not paid. I remember coming home and flipping the light switch only to discover that the lights had been turned off. I even remember looking in the kitchen pantry only to find a loaf of bread, some crackers, and about ten packages of ramen noodles. The struggle was real, and for those who can relate, y'all know that ramen goes for about six or seven packages for a dollar.

One meal I made during hard times was called "po' man's pancakes." I don't know if anyone has made them before, but it was by far the simplest thing that could be made when you only had a loaf of bread, butter, and some syrup at the house. The quick recipe goes as follows: Melt the butter in the skillet and then you butter and brown both sides of the bread. After you're done with a few slices, you drown them in syrup or jelly if you have it. Note to reader: boiling some water and adding some white or brown sugar can make syrup. This dish covered all the meals—breakfast, lunch, after-school snack, and even dinner. Even in the midst of those hard times, we still had God and each other, and we knew things wouldn't always be this way.

We were always happy 'cause we had our peace of

mind. We attended Love the Lord Church. Pastor Miller was our teacher. Pastor Miller was a man of God like no other. For me, he brought the Bible to life. It wasn't just the traditional teachings of most pastors, preachers, or ministers. He put scriptural teachings into real-life situations. He made the Bible applicable to everyday life. This type of teaching made me become interested in learning about God and the Bible. This was a change from what I was used to, as I had always been reared in an environment where I was forbidden to attend church. Since I never had the chance to join or even attend a non-denominational church, I had already formed within my mind that this was a bad place for me to go. Pastor Miller and the rest of the LTLC family were able to change my views about church and about God.

Mom had begun to rely heavily on God and prayer, because Granddad's health had spiraled downward significantly. Mom had started bringing him to the VA, the Veteran's Affairs Hospital, to receive treatment for the pain. In July of 1995, Granddad was diagnosed with prostate cancer. Granddad would often try to hide his pain from Mom. He had been living with the pain for sometime before the diagnosis, but it has now reached a point to where it was unbearable. While receiving treatment at the VA, Granddad refused to eat any of their hospital food. His favorite food could be found just a few streets up from the hospital at none other than Sweet Georgia Brown. Sweet Georgia Brown apparently served the best soul food in Dallas. On Sundays there was always a line of people wrapped around the building. You know people love to eat after hearing the Word. I was never a real fan of soul food, so I would only eat the dessert from there. They had the best peach cobbler. This peach cobbler was so good it'd make you wanna slap yo' mamma! I really enjoyed being around Granddad, and he seemed to be happiest when he was at the restaurant. Now don't let that fool you, Granddad was no stranger to the kitchen himself.

Ever since I can remember, the family would gather at his house on Saturday mornings for his famous chicken wings and biscuits. Granddad made the best wings and biscuits. The biscuits were so soft they would practically melt in your mouth and you know he made them from scratch. Those who have really been paying attention will note this is second time I've mentioned those wings and biscuits, so you know them biscuits were the bomb. When our family started growing apart I really missed this. Looking at Granddad now, you could see he wasn't the vibrant, vivacious person that he once was, that time had passed. Granddad didn't outwardly show his sickness, but you could see it in his eyes. I liked looking in Granddad's eyes for two reasons: one, they were hazel; and two, they looked as though they held a lifetime of stories and wisdom. As his visits to our home in Garland became more frequent, I grew accustomed to hearing the name "Cluck" coming from Mom's room, as she gave up her room for him when he was in town. Cluck was Granddad's nickname for Mom. To this day I don't know why he called her that. I guess it was a "country thang." Mom tried her best not to allow his sickness to affect her, but she had developed a special bond with him. Their bond had become stronger through the trials and tribulations that had transpired in Mom's life. This was especially evident during the points when she was most devastated—the divorce, and the death of Granny.

All the things he experienced during his sickness affected her. I would often hear her cry at night. Mom and Granddad shared a bond he didn't have with his other children. Mom was willing to sacrifice her time and energy to ensure his safety and care, while his other children would barely lift a finger. Mom's life was shattered when he died.

I remember it like it was yesterday. It was December of 1995 and I was visiting Dad for Christmas break. I was playing Mega Man 7 with Tyrone at Aunt Alberta's house. I was playing the Springman stage when the phone rang.

"Christopher, come to the phone, it's your mother."

I answered the phone with a certain excitement in my voice. "Hi, Mom."

Mom was quiet, so I knew something was wrong. Mom was always happy when we spoke on the phone. "Christopher, Granddad died t'day."

"When?!"

"About five o'clock today."

"Mom, just let me know if you need anything and I'll be there. I'll come back early to be with you after the funeral."

"Christopher, we'll be down there in few days. The family is all here, so I'll talk to you later."

As I hung up the phone, tears began to run down my cheeks. Aunt Alberta, realizing something was wrong, came over to comfort me. "Baby, it'll be all right. It was his time. Would you prefer for him to live in this world full of hurt and pain?"

"No."

"When's the funeral?"

"I don't know. I know it will have to be before Christmas. Mom will let me know tomorrow." I was really worried about Mom. She had been planning something special for Granddad on Christmas, but he never made it. The interesting thing was that he died with a smile on his face. It was as if he were happy to leave this place. He was pronounced dead on December 20, 1995. I knew it was going to be a chore for Mom to get the family together for this event. It's not easy to pull together quarreling brothers and sisters, even during a funeral. My Granddad didn't have many things, but what he owned was considered antique. Luann, Mom's older sister, was a crafty-one of sorts, and knew exactly what she was coming to accomplish. She wanted any and everything perceived to have antique value. Luann was an old, embittered woman, who was nosy. God, was she nosy! Not to mention, she talked to people like they had tails. She was not nice at all. She was plump, stuck-up, and mean. She had been the executrix of Granny's estate and she played the part. She wanted to go shopping in Granddad's house for antiques. She had nerves of steel to take from Granddaddy and his children like that since she wasn't even one of his own children. She was from Granny's first marriage. Mom was too busy to worry about her, but she knew what Aunt Luann was doing. Aunt Luann wasn't on my list of favorite aunts because of her recent actions at Sister Giovanni's. Mom's church sister, Sister Giovanni, had invited Mom and Aunt Luann over to spend the night, and during the course of the night Sister Giovanni discovered Aunt Luann searching through her drawers and closets. Sister Giovanni demanded that Luann be removed from her house immediately. In the midst of everything Mom had to endure, she now had to add embarrassment to a long list of unwanted emotions. This wasn't just Mom's friend, but this was a sister that she fellowshipped with at church.

Aunt Luann wasn't the only sibling acting a fool. Raymond, Mom's older brother, was an alcoholic. Uncle Ray would show up at family events, including funerals, a little toasted. I guess everyone, including me, put his or her feelings aside since his alcoholism came as a result of having fought in Vietnam. The war changed him. He left home as a boy and came home a broken man. Mom told me that the war stole his soul; it took over his life, as it did to most of the men who fought in it. Despite her siblings' personal problems, Mom fought to bring her divided family together no matter what. Granddad deserved that much.

At the service, I remember sitting behind Mom in the seats reserved for the family thinking, why? Why was Aunt Luann trying to out-sing the designated funeral singer? She tried, but Aunt Luann just didn't have it. Why did Uncle Ray come to the funeral saturated with the smell of beer? I was so embarrassed. I could feel the eyes of the other people in attendance focused at our family. Granddad's death only made Mom stronger. Mom had endured personal pains I can't even fathom. She survived losing both parents, colon cancer, giving up her oldest son, an adulterous husband, and finally, divorce. I admired her courage. Following Mom's example just a few months prior to Granddad's passing, I too, summoned my strength.

I was a freshman in high school, but my issues were deep and growing daily. I was always a non-athletic boy, but this year I was determined to prove them wrong. I decided to play football. I had to prove to my fellow peers and family that I could be a boy like all the other boys. Upon my decision to play football, the word gay as it related to me, vanished. Life had begun to go in a different direction. Every time I lined up on the line in the hot sun, I thought of how my family and peers were waiting for me to give up and quit. I was determined not to throw in the towel. After I survived the first two months, I felt that my family gained more respect for me. It is sad, but true. You grow up believing your family, above all others, is where you turn to for strength, but mine drained me of mine. Their thoughts and feelings had already done enough damage and I decided to close that chapter, and rely on my own inner strength. The statements they said caused me to question myself, and that wasn't healthy. Football was my salvation from this. At least, that's what I thought at the time. At thirteen, the easy answers like submitting to the societal "boy-like" norms where commonly accepted and easier to execute for me.

Football was the simple solution to my problems. Everything started looking better. I was on my way to being accepted as part of the in-crowd. For once, I actually felt like the other kids. I was able to stay on balance because of God and Mom. Dad was around, but visits became less frequent when he was placed on mandatory child support. He could no longer withhold funds because they were extracted from his check. That check saved us several times. I remember waiting for the check to come so we could get some food. Sitting around waiting for a check to tide us over until Mom got paid was quite difficult at times. I knew that just about every other Wednesday the check would be in the mailbox. Sometimes the check would arrive a week or so late. I hated waiting for that check. I would often get mad at Dad because it would come late. In reality, I should have been mad at the postman for always delivering it late instead of Dad, since

71

it was automatically taken out of his check. The check wasn't much, but it was necessary to help provide extra funds for household expenses. I had grown to accept this fact since I never received the whole amount of the check to use for my own disposal. I felt that it was being used for greater good, but oftentimes it was spent on miscellaneous stuff. Mom had a very big heart in the church, so often the check would go for a special offering when we didn't have groceries in the house. Mom knew and felt deep within that she would receive her blessings from God. I could not understand this reasoning, but I didn't have much say in the matter. I felt like it was okay to give tithes and offerings, but don't overdo it to the point where you have to do without. Mom's giving paid off though, in more ways than one. As I began to be confronted with emotions like denial and confusion in my sleep through never-ending dreams, or for me, daily nightmares, I saw how she depended on Him for everything, so I began to pray more and ask for guidance from Him before I slept.

I never had dealt with myself by actually processing my true thoughts and internal feelings in such a real way before, so this was extremely difficult. I faced questions in my dreams like, why don't I have a girlfriend? and why am I still affected by the thoughts and feelings of others? The whispers had stopped long ago, but somehow they had seeped into my mind, body, and soul. It was as though I didn't have a choice anymore. I was doomed to live as labeled by the gossip. Who was I becoming? Mom didn't recognize the changes because she was at work all the time, and while she was there I managed to conjure up enough strength to put my carnal desires on a back burner. I eventually got to a point to where I sealed those thoughts and feelings within the far reaches of mind, never to be released. I became more actively involved in school and church to help keep my mind occupied. I was a youth minister at Love the Lord, so I immersed myself in the Bible. I became consumed with studying and learning the Word that I forgot about the reflection I had seen in the mirror. The image of myself I saw reflected in the mirror was someone I was determined not to be. I did not want to be gay. Mom looked at the recent changes in church as a positive thing. I ran from this gay person, and the only time he would catch me was when I was asleep. I would have nightmares and tremors of being the gay one in the family. This was not for me. This could not be me.

Remember Tyson? Well, he was a freshman in college now. He attended San Almeda State University (SASU) on a full athletic scholarship. Mom was very proud of Tyson. He had managed to turn a bad situation into a good one. However, as he attended school, he made Mom suffer. Tyson ran up numerous calls on her calling card that was only supposed to be used to call home. Tyson never called home. Mom allowed him to get away with it, probably out of some misguided guilt, and he continued. I guess Mom felt since she had opted to allow Uncle Vincent and Aunt Eloise to finish raising him that she owed him something. In a sense, I felt that was the way Tyson perceived things as well. He felt the world owed him something for going through this life and its many complications.

In February of 1996, Mom received a phone call from Aunt Eloise. She told Mom to speak with Tyson about his grades. Tyson was about to flunk out of school. After the conversation, Mom hung up the phone with a disappointed and disheartened look in her eyes. It was as though she were doubtful of the information, but had no choice but to believe it coming from Aunt Eloise. I am sure thoughts of how, or why would Tyson allow this circled in and out of her consciousness before anger registered.

Mom then turned to me and said, "How dare they keep Tyson's life secret until he gets in trouble!" Mom could never get them to divulge any information about Tyson, and now all of the sudden they wanted to include her in his life. True enough, Tyson's grades had slipped. His GPA was a little above 1.0. Tyson had found other things to occupy his time. Mom immediately began calling SASU to check on him. She learned that Tyson was basically taking basket-weaving classes. There was not one core class, like English or math on his class roster. He didn't want to be in school. After speaking with counselors and professors on Tyson's behalf, he was placed on academic probation. This didn't last long, because in April, Tyson was dismissed from the school.

Tyson was sent to jail for some type of criminal activity, and SASU released him as a result. I still don't know the exact nature of the crime to this day. Mom, Dad, and I paid $1,000 together to post his bond. Tyson came back to Garland to live with us. This was a mandate within his probation. Tyson often lied about his convictions. It was always some different, elaborate story each day. He would often come home reeking of alcohol. When Tyson drank he became disrespectful to Mom and me. It made me angry, because Mom would just allow it. She felt that she had failed him as a parent. Mom prayed for him every night. She was determined to keep what was left of her family together. She had already lost so much, she couldn't lose us too. It was as though this was her second chance to correct past faux pas. Mom continued to allow this constant disrespect until Tyson left.

"Tyson, where are you going?"

"I'm leaving, Momma!" Tyson yelled.

"Tyson, please don't leave, your blood is on my hands!" Mom pleaded.

"Mom, I'm not a kid anymore. Quit trying to hold my hand. I free you of this responsibility. I can take care of myself. Bye."

"Tyson, wait!"

CHAPTER 6

PEACE BE STILL...

I pray that peace be amongst my family in years to come. Most of all, I pray for strength, unity, and love.

After Tyson left, Mom went through a very tough time. It was as though she were looking through a window at something that belonged to her, and for some reason she was unable to reach it. There was always a prayer in Mom's heart for Tyson. Oftentimes these very prayers probably saved his life. Again, I had to watch Mom experience a loss. Tyson had pretty much disowned us all in the midst of what was a new chapter in my life.

I was a sophomore in the fall of 1996. Life was quite different this year. In light of my previous bout with football, I had decided to play another year. I had nothing to prove to anyone. Mom and I certainly had our share of issues this year. It was as though we were meant to weather through the storms. Withstanding all that came our way made us grow together. Unity was the word of the year. Mom had recently gotten in a wreck in her new 1995 Sonata. The guy who hit her skipped town. He was in his company's truck, but Mom didn't know where to turn for help. She called on Sister Giovanni, and she recommended a lawyer to her. Mom visited the lawyer and gave him all the information she had on the person involved in the incident. In the end, the lawyer decided not to represent her. He stated it was too much risk for him to try to tackle it. Mom was left car-less, without anyone to defend her. She was disappointed, but not too broken as this outcome was all too commonplace. Mom moved on from this incident. This was just another page in her book of disappointments and sorrow. The pain and suffering she endured from the accident helped me come to a conclusion. I would never let her down, even if it meant I had to close the door on myself. Mom needed and deserved to be first in someone's life and I wanted her to be first in mine. I never really fit in with anyone, mainly because I lived a façade. The façade was created to avoid dealing with the "me" on the inside, and now I had justified the façade because I couldn't burden Mom.

Back at school the Scholastic Aptitude Test (SAT) was approaching. I was always academically inclined, so without preparation I decided to take the SAT. Luckily I scored in the average percentile on the first try. It wasn't a very high score, but I was just glad to have completed the test. It's a little bit weird to finish a test unknown to me, but fail at life's test. People never saw it in me, but I saw my life as a failure and ran from the problems that needed solving. Why was I running? I ran every day in football practice, you'd think that would have been enough. The sport wasn't in my heart, but somehow it made me feel needed. I felt happy being a significant part of group. I never gave my all to football practice; I only did enough to be accepted. It was as though I were giving up without giving up. Football started to become the place where I was confronted by my internal desires even while awake. This happened day in and day out. I remember back to my freshman year, when it all began…

I was standing in line waiting for the sports' doctor to give me a physical. The doctor made us all strip down to our skin, and we were seen five at a time. I felt awkward and I broke out in a cold sweat. The only thing I remember was that physically, mentally, and emotionally I changed. Being in a room full of naked bodies, an appendage rose to the occasion and there was no hiding it. It had finally caught up with me. With my pants off I was stripped of everything but my innocence. After a time, my innocence was lost as well, my mind forever left corrupted. I was left pondering what could be, and how should I behave.

This football year was better than the previous year. I perfected my "game face," you know, the face you want your opponents to see, strong and intimidating. Football can teach you so much. In the game you also get to wear a helmet for added protection. Well, I transferred these rules over to everyday life, wearing my game face for protection from anyone who got too close. No one ever knew the turmoil inside me. I was struggling with issues that had been in me for years but I went to class day in and day out, and from there I went to football practice like nothing was wrong. We practiced very hard this year, and for this we were rewarded. We became the district champs for this year. With a nine-to-one season, my football career could not have been better. During the off-season I started contemplating my future. What, where, and who would I be in two years? five years? Would I attend college, and what would I major in? What path would I take?

I was probably the only student in the entire school with these types of thoughts. I began to buckle down and look deep within, and by January of 1997 I found the answers to my questions. I decided to graduate early and attend Howard University. I planned to major in biological science or pre-medicine. When I spoke about these things most of my family were supportive of my endeavors. In the far reaches of my mind I wondered if this was the truth I visualized. Mom never doubted me. I turned this into my inner strength. Dad was busy trying to relive his own failed football career through me, so he wanted me to stay in high school an extra year to play football. The only thing I could think of was getting away. I felt caged here. I needed to spread my wings. After passing the TAAS test I made preparations to go to summer school. I needed to take English IV to advance to senior status the following year. Mom supported me two hundred and ten percent in all my decisions. Next thing I knew, it was summer, time to set things in motion.

I sat in a classroom surrounded by people who had failed the class during the standard school year. During our introduction, the teacher asked us to reveal our age, how many times we had taken the class, and any other interesting facts about ourselves. As I listened to each person, I distinctly remember laughing inside at one guy. He began to share his story, and I drifted off into dreamland. I awoke at the end of his speech when he stated, "I'm twenty-one, and this is my fourth time taking this course." I instantly thought, My God! What an imbecile. I later learned that he wasn't dumb or ignorant, and many family problems had altered his path. He had nowhere to live at present because his father had kicked him out. He also revealed to me that his father physically abused his mother. His mother left out of fear, only she forgot one thing—him. I was astounded by the fact that a mother could actually allow herself to leave a child, especially one of her blood, in an abusive environment. I thought that was very selfish of her. I began to reflect on my own situation, and I felt blessed to be free of the verbal abuse that Dad had chosen to share with all the members of our family. I felt even more blessed to know that I had a mother who cared enough about me not to leave me stranded so she could pursue her own freedom. After the first day we never spoke again. A few days later he never came back to school. I could only hope that he was safe. This just goes to show that you never know the cards that will be dealt in life. Not everyone is given a winning hand. I excelled in summer school. I passed the class with a ninety-eight, and later that summer I began yet another transformation.

The person in the mirror was beginning to intrigue me. Not the person I let the world see, but the real me. I became a prisoner of my own lustful desires. The desires disseminated from my interior man to my exterior man. I began to move away from my foundation, which was at the time based on my relationship with my church. I knew I had lost the "old me" when I attempted to perform the very act that I had long denied was even possible to everyone, including myself. I created a whirlwind of words to convince my classmate to experiment with me. I simply overwhelmed my classmate to do my bidding. Anything I asked, my classmate did. I would often have to go to work in the midst of our curious play, so I could only explore my desires for a few hours. Oh, by the way, after summer school Little Caesar's Pizza hired me. I had recently turned sixteen, and my adventures were truly beginning. How can you be taken over? By accepting the truth—that you've given in. I knew I was tired of fighting it. I now worked for it, instead of it trying so hard to work at capturing me. I was captured and enraptured in it.

With the start of my senior year, I was so happy to

be graduating in the spring. I had applied to attend Howard University, and in November 1997 I was accepted. The school offered me no financial assistance, so I knew I had difficult road ahead. This was my senior year, and I was determined to make it memorable. So I made sure I attended the first dance of year, homecoming. I went solo, but it was cool. I dressed down. I had on black slacks, some freshly buffed black shoes, a white shirt, a royal purple, black, and white tie, and to top it all off, a royal purple, polyester blend jacket. I was too handsome for my own good. I felt good even though I didn't have a date. I didn't have much rhythm, so I just stood around. I turned down several dances to save me the embarrassment. The highlight of my night was sitting around eating cookies, drinking punch, and standing against the wall in the cafeteria-turned-dance hall. I left after two hours. I told Mom a lot of fictitious stories about the evening, so that I would not look like a "square" to her. Mom was quite the socialite during her high school career. I was always an introverted child, so social gatherings made me feel out of place.

The next school day, I had somehow developed friends. I wasn't one to just talk to everyone, but I always treated people fairly. One set of newly found friends stood out from them all. They were two sisters named Shonda and Delia. They had recently transferred from North Wind High School in Worthwood. I remember talking with them one day as we were heading to the school bus after school. Shonda mentioned that I resembled someone that had graduated from their old school when they were freshmen. Shonda turned to me and said, "You know, Christopher, you look like this guy that used to go to my old high school. I think his name was Tyson Coldwell."

I replied, "Huh? Man, Shonda, that's my older brother."

"Hey, Delia guess what?"

"What, Shonda?"

"Christopher is Tyson's little brother!"

"For real?! You playing."

"Nah, she right Delia, Tyson is my older brother."

"You know Shonda, he does favor Tyson a lot."

I was actually shocked that someone at this school knew my brother. We instantly had a connection because we both knew Tyson. Shonda and I were just friends, but some of the guys and girls around the school thought it was more. Some of the guys at school were jealous of me, because Shonda was one of the best looking females in the entire school, and she was new. Most of them felt she would fall prey to their games, since she didn't know their past. However, I was a friend who didn't mind sharing the information I had on them. As our friendship progressed, I developed a crush on her, but I was too chicken to pursue it. I was afraid that she would reject me. I just kept my attraction in the far reaches of my mind. Time passed and it came time for another dance to occur. I swallowed my fears and asked to escort her to the Legend Dance. Surprisingly, she said, "Yes, Christopher, I will go to Legend with you."

This was my first dance where I had a date, so I had to make everything special. Mom rented us a limousine for the night. We had talked several times about the attire we would have on, so our dress complimented one another. I had this big limousine with only three people riding in it. Shonda, Delia, and I rode to the dance in style. I was so happy to be at the dance with someone instead of being alone. Caught up in the atmosphere of everything, I just drifted away. I forgot that I didn't know how to dance. Luckily, Mom had taught me a simple side-to-side slow dance a few years back. This was my night to bask in joy and happiness. I felt that being here with her was the best possible thing in the world. I managed to step on her toes quite a few times. I apologized, but I was so happy not even those incidents could bring me down. Shonda was understanding. After that night, I just smiled in reverie when I thought of the events of that evening. This feeling lasted for about three weeks, until the phone rang one evening after school.

"Hello." There was an automated voice on the line. "This is MCI and we have a collect call from—"

"Tyson."

"Will you accept? If yes, say yes after the tone or just push one."

I pushed one on the phone. "What's up, Tyson?"

"I need you to call Dad, because I'm in jail."

"What?! I mean, what happened, Tyson?"

"Hey man, I'll tell you later, just call Dad, and tell Mom."

It seemed as though during the entire course of the conversation time stood still. I knew something was terribly wrong, I just didn't know how to go about resolving it. Mom came in from work a few minutes after I hung up the phone, and before I could sit her down and tell her, the phone rang. It was Tyson once again. As Mom and Tyson talked, it was as though a part of her soul were being ripped from her body. Mom grew terribly silent after she hung up the phone. Tears began to roll down her cheeks. "What am I going to do, Christopher?"

"I don't know, Momma."

"All I can say is call Daddy and pray."

"Mom, what happened to Tyson? Why is he in there again?"

"Christopher, Tyson didn't tell me the entire story, but I do know that he's violated his probation."

This was the second time I was present to witness Mom's countenance fall. In the weeks following, Mom worked with Dad to try to get Tyson out, but they only had failed attempts. Tyson was going to have to serve some time behind bars for violating his probation. This was just a fact. Mom went to visit Tyson a few times. She could only see and hear her son, now behind bulletproof glass. I knew Mom cried every time she left the facilities. When she would walk through the door I could see the remnants of pain staining her delicate face. Her nose was red and she had little to say. We never went into depth about the hurt Mom now faced, but I could see it all too well when I looked into her eyes.

My senior year progressed, and I was left to deal with myself. Mom and I didn't have many open-air conversations anymore. We became as ghosts, two spirits never truly touching. As the final months, weeks, and days counted away, I grew distant from my senior class. I did not feel part of class until I marched in Autumn Coliseum. At graduation, surrounded by family, I still felt alone. I could feel deep within that Tyson was with me every step of the way even though he wasn't here physically. I felt his presence all around me. I knew my wings had begun to spread. There were life challenges left to face, yet I knew them not. What would become of me? What was next, and would I survive? This is my story, and I have only spoken these words as a boy-turned-man.

###

WINGS

White, fluffy, and soft

What are wings?

Freedom, soaring, tranquility

. . .

Oh how I love to soar high above the clouds,

Please my dear sweet son, don't fly too close to sun,

Your wings will melt if you do

. . .

What happens when we have no freedom?

What happens when we can no longer soar?

What happens when wings melt?

WHEN WINGS MELT

In this cold and dark hotel room, all one could hear is the gentle whirr of the ceiling fan above. The room, a suite, decorated with contemporary Asian-inspired art and modern bamboo fixtures.

Man it's super early I thought as I hugged the pillow extra-tight before the alarm buzzed for the third time.

Quickly fading back into my 5 minute slumber, I think…How did I get here? What did I do to deserve this? You are fuckin' 28 years old.

What in the hell is going on in your life!? How will I tell mom, dad…Tyson? You are better than this Chris, you are better than this …

…(alarm buzzes)…

To be continued…

FROM THE AUTHOR

So many of us go through things in our lives, but as the old saying goes, "If it does not kill you, it can only make you stronger. " I am here to tell you that we all must go through the valleys, but know one thing, He will be with you always. Remember this as we begin a new era in our life, keep your head up and always look to the hills as your help is near even in your darkest hour. So with that being said, love one another and do not forget that there's always a rainbow at the end of our storm.

www.ingramcontent.com/pod-product-compliance
Lightning Source LLC
Chambersburg PA
CBHW071337130626
46556CB00004B/1928